Peter Sís

AN OCEAN WORLD

Greenwillow Books
An Imprint of HarperCollins*Publishers*

Pen and ink and watercolor paints were used for the full-color art.
The text type is ITC Modern No. 216.

An Ocean World
Copyright © 1992 by Peter Sís
All rights reserved.
Printed in the United States of America.
www.harperchildrens.com

Library of Congress Cataloging-in-Publication Data
Sís, Peter.
An ocean world.
p.   cm.
"Greenwillow Books."
Summary: A whale sails new seas and,
after several unsuccessful attempts, makes a friend.
ISBN 0-688-09067-2 (trade).
ISBN 0-688-09068-0 (lib. bdg.)–ISBN 0-688-17518-X (pbk.)
[1. Whales–Fiction.   2. Stories without words.]
I. Title. PZ7.S62190c 1992 [E]–dc20 89-11692 CIP AC

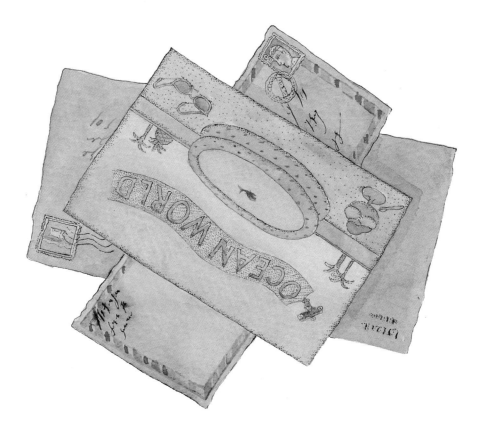

To all who care about our world

Greetings from Ocean World!
This morning I saw a whale
who has been here since she
was just a few weeks old.
Soon the day will come when
she will be returned to the ocean
to live with others of her kind.
She has seen many people but has
never seen another whale. I wonder
what it will be like for her!

Love
Peter

FAMILY SIS

9 BLEECKER ST. #21

NEW YORK

NY 10012

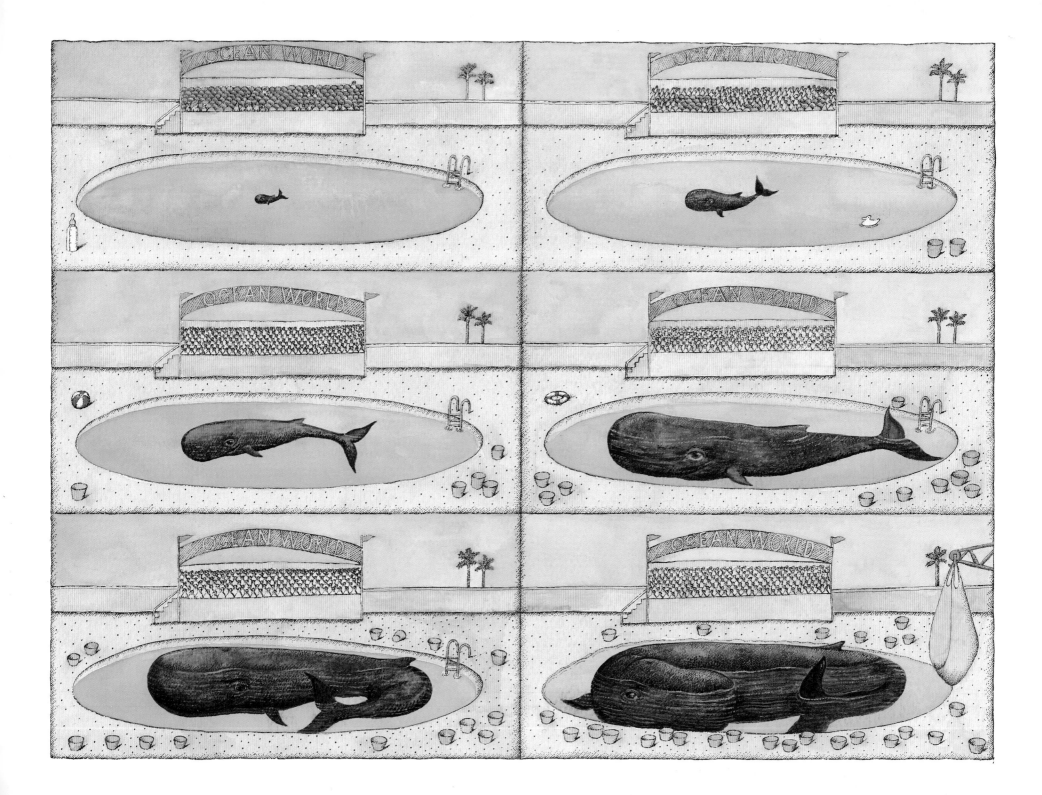

The whale grew

and

grew

and

grew

until...

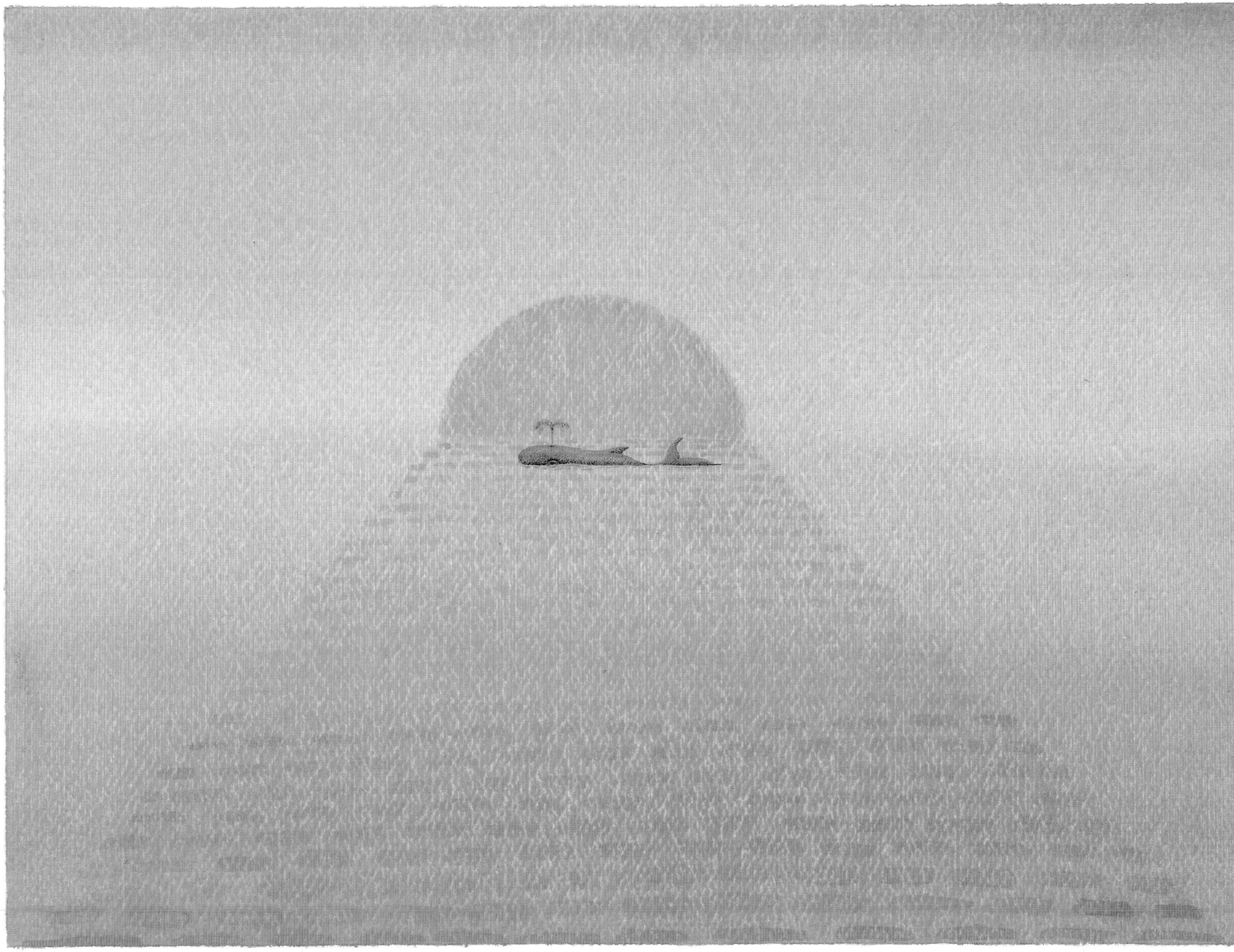

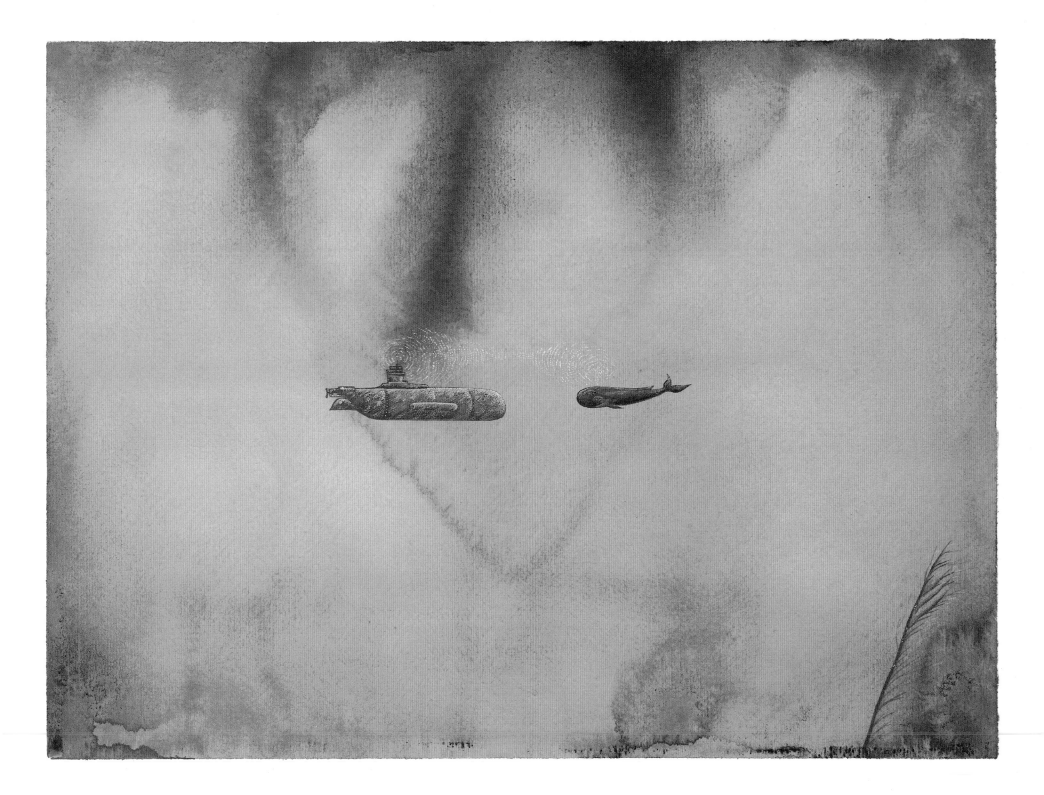

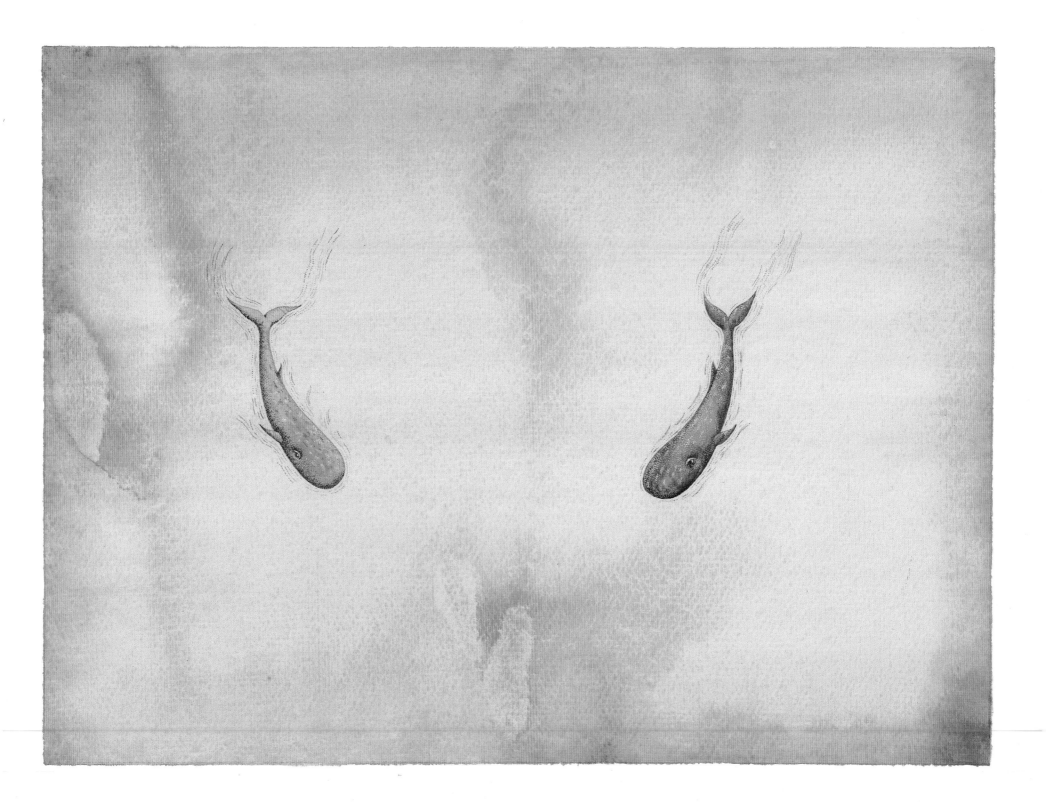